This Topsy and Tim book belongs to

_____

Topsy and Tim
Go for Gold

By Jean and Gareth Adamson

Illustrations by Belinda Worsley

A catalogue record for this book is available from the British Library

Published by Ladybird Books Ltd
A Penguin Company
Penguin Books Ltd., 80 Strand, London WC2R 0RL, UK
Penguin Books Australia Ltd., Camberwell, Victoria, Australia
Penguin Group (NZ) 67 Apollo Drive, Rosedale, North Shore 0632, New Zealand

001 –
1 3 5 7 9 10 8 6 4 2

ISBN: 978-1-40930-946-8
Printed in China

www.topsyandtim.com

Topsy and Tim were very excited. There
was going to be a Sports Day at school.
"I'm going to win a gold medal because I'm
the fastest runner in the class," said Tim.
"No you're not," said Topsy. "I am."

Topsy and Tim went into their garden to practise racing. Topsy won the first race and Tim won the second, but only because he pushed Topsy.

Topsy was so cross that she kicked Tim. It was lucky she was wearing soft trainers.
"Children, children!" said Mummy, as she sorted them out. "Sports Days are meant to be fun."

Sports Day was bright and sunny,
but Topsy and Tim were not.
"Oh dear!" said Miss Terry. "It isn't
like you to fall out, Topsy and Tim."

"They can't decide which of them can run faster,"
explained Mummy.
"Well, we can soon find out," said Miss Terry.
"The running race is about to start."

Topsy and Tim stood in line with the rest of their class. Miss Terry called, "Ready . . . Steady . . . GO!" and the children raced away as fast as they could.

Topsy ran so fast that she tripped over her toes.
Tim looked back to make sure he was winning and
he tripped over his heels.
"Never mind," said Miss Terry. "There are plenty
more races."

Miss Terry began to arrange an obstacle race. She put out a row of hoops . . . a row of upside-down buckets . . . and a row of chairs.

On each chair stood a cup of water and a ping-pong bat.

The children each grabbed a hoop, wriggled through it, then tossed their hoops over the buckets. But Topsy and Tim tried to wriggle through the same hoop.

Next they had to crawl under the chairs without upsetting the cups of water. Topsy and Tim did that quite well.

Last of all they raced to the finishing tape with the cups of water balanced on their ping-pong bats. Everyone got rather wet and Rai won the race.

The sack race was fun. Miss Terry couldn't tell which was Topsy and which was Tim. They had pulled their sacks up over their heads.

Tony won the sack race by jumping all the way.

Topsy and Tim loved the dressing-up race.
The children had to put on funny old clothes and
big shoes, then run along with their umbrellas up.

Topsy and Tim could not get their umbrellas
to go up, so they came last in that race.
"Stupid umbrellas!" grumbled Topsy.

"The next races are egg and spoon races for the mums and dads," said the headmaster, Mr Taylor, in a loud voice. Topsy and Tim pulled their mummy to the starting line.

All the children cheered as their mums raced for the winning tape. They all ran very fast, but some of them dropped their eggs. Topsy and Tim were amazed to see their mummy win.

Miss Terry was looking for pairs of children to run in the three-legged race.

"We must have you, Topsy and Tim," said Miss Terry. "You are a pair already."

She tied Tim's left leg to Topsy's right leg.

Some of the children in the race were big and some were small. They did not make neat pairs.

Topsy and Tim were twins. They were exactly the same size. They ran easily while the others struggled. "We're going to win!" shouted Topsy and Tim. And so they did.

Mr Taylor presented golden medals to all the winners of the races. He gave Topsy and Tim each a medal, because they had won the three-legged race together.

"Well, Topsy and Tim," said Miss Terry.
"Now do you know which of you can run faster?"
"We both can," said Topsy and Tim.

Now turn the page and help
Topsy and Tim solve a puzzle.

Topsy and Tim and little Stevie Dunton are practising for a race. Can you follow the lines and work out which of them crosses the finish line first?

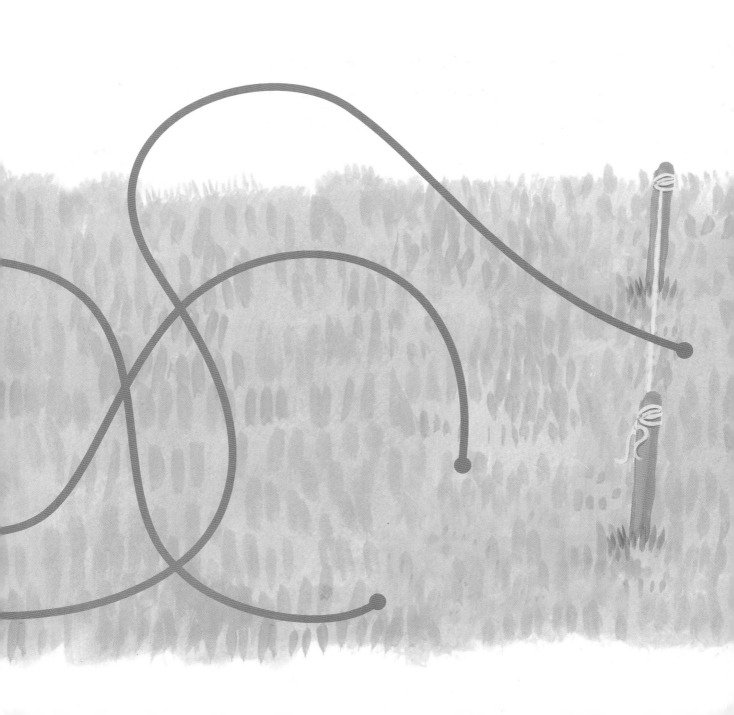

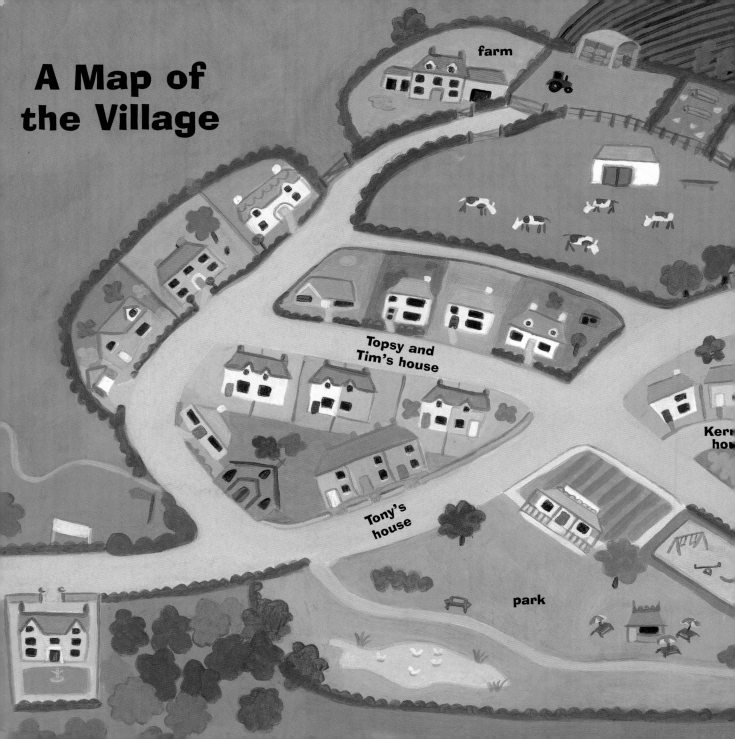

A Map of the Village

farm

Topsy and
Tim's house

Tony's
house

Kerr
hou

park

garage

post office

health centre

church

primary school

nursery school

police station

Have you read all the Topsy and Tim stories?

    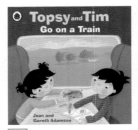

 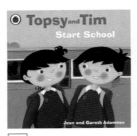 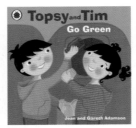  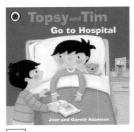

 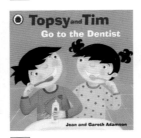   

  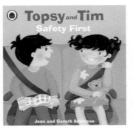 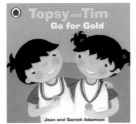 

 The Ladybird Topsy and Tim app can be downloaded from the App Store.